For Anna
– SS

To Mum, Dad and his delicious vegetable soup
– JD

LITTLE TIGER PRESS LTD
an imprint of the Little Tiger Group
1 Coda Studios
189 Munster Road, London SW6 6AW
www.littletiger.co.uk

First published in Great Britain 2006
This edition published 2018

A CIP catalogue record for this book is available
from the British Library

CD contains:
1 - complete story with original music and sound effects
2 - story with page turn pings to encourage learner readers to join in

Running time over 15 mins
Music composed by Mark Bates
Story read by Anna Crace
This recording copyright © Little Tiger Press 2018
℗ Mark Bates

ISBN 978-1-84869-865-9
LTP/1800/2260/0218
Printed in China
10 9 8 7 6 5 4 3 2 1

THE LAMB WHO CAME FOR DINNER

STEVE SMALLMAN   JOËLLE DREIDEMY

LITTLE TIGER
LONDON

"Vegetable soup AGAIN!"
moaned the old wolf. "Oh,
I wish I had a little lamb.
I could make a hotpot.
my favourite!"
    Just then . . . .

KNOCK!
KNOCK!

It was a little lamb.
"Can I come in?"
the little lamb said.
"Yes, my dear, do
come in. You're just
in time for dinner!"
sniggered the old
wolf.

The little lamb was shivering with cold.
BRRRR! BRRRR! she went.
"GOODNESS GRACIOUS ME!" said the old wolf. "I can't eat a lamb that's frozen. I HATE frozen food!"

So he put her next to the fire to thaw her out.

The old wolf looked up a recipe for lamb hotpot. Mmmmmm! He felt hungry just at the thought of it.

The lamb was feeling hungry
too. Her tummy rumbled.
RUMBLE! RUMBLE! it went.
   "GOODNESS GRACIOUS ME!"
said the old wolf. "I can't eat a
lamb with a rumbling tummy.
I might get indigestion!"

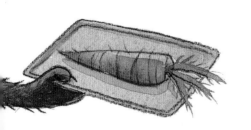

So he gave the lamb
a carrot to eat. "Stuffing,"
he said to himself.

The little lamb gobbled
down the carrot so quickly
that she got hiccups!

HIC,
HIC,
HICCUP!

she went.

"GOODNESS GRACIOUS
ME!" said the old wolf.
"I can't eat a lamb with
hiccups! I might catch
them too!"

But he didn't know
how to cure hiccups.

He tried throwing the
lamb up in the air.

HIC!

That didn't work.

He held her
upside-down.

HIC!

That didn't work.

He twirled her
round and round.

HICCUP!

That didn't work either!

So the old wolf put the lamb over
his shoulder and patted her back with
his big hairy paw.

The lamb stopped hiccupping, snuggled
under the old wolf's shaggy chin and fell
fast asleep in his arms. The old wolf felt
funny. He'd never been hugged by his
dinner before and suddenly he didn't feel
so hungry after all.

The little lamb snored gently in his ear.
SNORE! SNORE! she went.

"Goodness gracious me!" whispered the
old wolf. "I can't eat a lamb that's snoring!"

He sniffed, then sniffed again. The little lamb smelt so . . . so . . . DELICIOUS! "Oh!" groaned the wolf. "If I eat her quickly, it'll be all right." And he was just about to gobble her up when . . .

The old wolf sat down in the chair by the fire, the little lamb warm on his chest, and thought just how very long it had been since anyone had given him a cuddle.

. . . she woke up and gave
him a great big kiss.

SMACK!

"NOOO!!!"

howled the wolf,
"THAT'S NOT FAIR!
I am a big, bad WOLF
and you are . . . hotpot!"

"Hop-pop!" said the little
lamb with a smile. Then
she pointed at the old
wolf and said, "Woof!"

"Oh, give me strength!"
groaned the old wolf.
"You'll have to go!"

He wrapped the little lamb
up warmly and put her
outside.
   "NOW GO AWAY!"
he shouted. "If you stay here,
I'll eat you, and then we'll
both be sorry!" And he shut
the door with a
                      BANG!

It was dark outside, and cold.
The little lamb banged on the door.
   "Woof?" she cried. "Can I come in, Woof?"
   But the old wolf stuck his fingers in his ears
and went "LA! LA! LA!" until she stopped.
   At last, all was quiet. "Thank goodness she's gone!"
thought the wolf. "She's not safe here with
a hungry old wolf like me."

Then he thought of
the lamb, all alone in
the dark wood.

"She might get lost!"

"She might get frozen!"

"She might get eaten!"

"OH NO, WHAT HAVE I DONE?"

he howled. He leapt up and opened the door.

The lamb was gone.

The old wolf rushed out into the
dark wood, crying, "Little lamb!
Little lamb! Come back!
I won't eat you . . . I promise!"

Much, much later, a sad, soggy old wolf trudged wearily back to his cottage alone.

He pushed open the door and there, by the fire, sat the little lamb!

"YOU CAME BACK!" said the wolf with a smile. "Haven't you got anywhere else to go?"

The little lamb shook her head.

"Er . . . er . . . then would you like to stay here . . . with me?" asked the wolf.

The little lamb gave him a hard stare. "Not eat me, Woof, no?" she said.

"GOODNESS GRACIOUS ME!" said the old wolf. "I can't eat a lamb who needs me! I might get heartburn!"

The little lamb smiled and then threw herself into the old wolf's arms.

"Are you feeling hungry, Hotpot?" asked the wolf.

"How about some vegetable soup?

It's my favourite."

More fabulous books from Little Tiger Press!

Old MacDino had a Farm
Becky Davies • Ben Whitehouse

BLUE MONSTER WANTS IT ALL!
JEANNE WILLIS • JENNI DESMOND

CoCk-a-dOoDle-POO!
Steve Smallman • Florence Weiser

NIBBLES The BOOK Monster
By EMMA YARLETT

FAIRY TALE PETS
TRACEY CORDEROY • JORGE MARTIN

CAN I JOIN YOUR CLUB?
John Kelly • Steph Laberis

For information regarding any of the above books or for our catalogue, please contact us:
Little Tiger Press, 1 Coda Studios, 189 Munster Road, London SW6 6AW
Tel: 020 7385 6333 • E-mail: contact@littletiger.co.uk • www.littletiger.co.uk